This Topsy and Tim
book belongs to

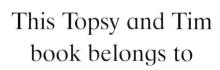

_____

Topsy + Tim

look after their pets

Jean and Gareth Adamson

All Ladybird books are available at most bookshops, supermarkets
and newsagents, or can be ordered direct from:
Ladybird Postal Sales PO Box 133 Paignton TQ3 2YP England
Telephone: (+44) 01803 554761   *Fax:* (+44) 01803 663394
A catalogue record for this book is available from the British Library

Published by Ladybird Books Ltd
A subsidiary of the Penguin Group
A Pearson Company

© Jean and Gareth Adamson MCMXCV
This edition MCMXCVIII

Topsy and Tim's smallest pet was
Tubby mouse. Tubby was really Tim's
mouse but Topsy played with him too.

Every evening, after school, Tim put a teaspoonful of crushed oats and sunflower seeds into Tubby's dish. Sometimes he gave Tubby treats, like a piece of bread soaked in milk or water, or bits of carrot or apple. Tubby liked his treats.

Tubby liked to play outside his cage.
Twice a week, Mummy helped Tim to
clean out the cage, while Topsy kept
an eye on Tubby. Mummy washed the
cage clean. Tim spread new sawdust
on the floor and put fresh hay in
Tubby's sleeping box.

'I'll fill Tubby's water bottle,'
said Topsy one evening.
'No,' said Tim. 'He's my mouse, so
I fill his water bottle.'
Topsy cupped her hands and gently
scooped Tubby up. 'I wish I had
a mouse,' she said.

'We don't want another mouse,'
said Mummy. 'They might have lots of
babies and we wouldn't be able to
look after them properly.'
'I'd look after them,' said Topsy.
'No,' said Mummy and that was that.

Topsy went to feed the goldfish,
Sam and Roundabout. Topsy liked them,
but they weren't as much fun as
a mouse.

Sam and Roundabout lived in a
proper, rectangular fish tank.
It stood in a shady corner of
the room. Dad had fixed some
water weed to small rocks with
elastic bands. Sam and Roundabout
liked to nibble the weed.

'Mummy,' said Topsy, 'the fish
need more water.'
Mummy floated a piece of clean
paper on the water.

She gave Topsy a jug of fresh water to pour gently on to the paper. 'That stops the tank getting stirred up,' she said.

Topsy filled the tank very
carefully. Then she took the
paper out. Sam and Roundabout
swam happily in their clean water.

Topsy gave them a little pinch
of fish food. She knew she mustn't
overfeed them.
'Don't forget to put the cover back
on the tank,' said Mummy. 'We don't
want Kitty to put her paw in and catch
them.'

Topsy and Tim went into the garden
to look after Wiggles, their black
and white rabbit.
'I'll put Wiggles in his run. Then
we can clean his cage,' said Tim.
'You mustn't pick him up by his ears,'
said Topsy.
'I know that!' said Tim.

Tim lifted Wiggles out of his cage
very carefully, keeping one hand
underneath, and put him safely in
his run.
Topsy cleaned out the hutch
and put in fresh straw.

Topsy filled Wiggles' dish with oats
and bran and put clean water in his
drinking bowl. Mummy gave Tim
some apple, carrots and lettuce leaves
to put in Wiggles' run.

While Topsy and Tim were playing
with Wiggles, Josie Miller came
to see them. She was carrying
her hamster cage.
'Please will you look after Lily
for me?' she said. 'I'm going
away on holiday for a week.'

Topsy and Tim ran to ask Mummy
if they could.
'All right,' said Mummy, 'but Josie
must tell you how to look after
a hamster.'

Josie gave them a packet of
hamster food. 'You must fill Lily's
dish every evening,' she said.
'She also likes bits of apple, carrot,
lettuce or cabbage, and she loves nuts!'

Just then, Lily popped out of her
nest box and went to her food dish.
'Isn't she eating a lot!' said Tim.
'She isn't eating it,' said Josie.
'She's filling the pouches in her cheeks.
Then she will put the food in her food
store to eat later.'

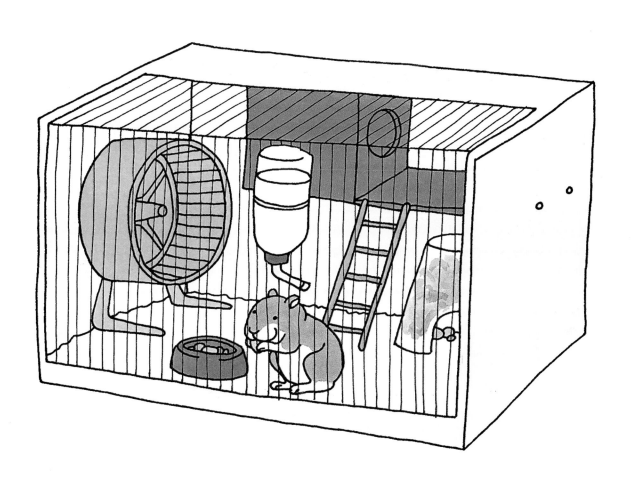

Josie asked Topsy and Tim to clean out Lily's food store every other day, so that it didn't get smelly. 'And please will you fill her water bottle every day,' said Josie.
'I'll do that!' said Topsy.

'She's got an exercise wheel like Tubby's,' said Tim.

'Yes,' said Josie. 'You'll hear her playing in it at night-time.'

Just then, Tubby climbed into his wheel and had a spin.

'Lily will have a lovely time
with Topsy and Tim and their pets,'
said Mummy.
'Goodbye, Lily,' said Josie. 'Have
a good holiday with Topsy and Tim!'